This igloo book belongs to:

....

igloobooks

Published in 2018
by Igloo Books Ltd
Cottage Farm
Sywell
NN6 0BJ
www.igloobooks.com

GOL002 0918
2 4 6 8 10 9 7 5 3 1
ISBN 978-1-78905-189-6

Written by Melanie Joyce
Illustrated by James Newman Gray

Designed by Kerri-Ann Hulme
Edited by Caroline Richards

Printed and manufactured in China

Night-time Bunny

igloobooks

Deep in the wood, in a snuggly burrow,
hungry Bunny was having his supper.
It was nearly bedtime and he was slurping
the last of his delicious carrot soup.

"Mummy, do all the animals in the wood
go to bed when it gets dark?" asked Bunny.
"No," said Mummy, "some of them sleep
during the day and wake up at night."

Bunny thought being awake at night sounded very exciting.
"Please can I see the animals that come out at night?"
he asked. "I want to be a night-time bunny!"

Mummy's knitting needles clicked and clacked.
"Okay," she said, putting her knitting down.
"Let's go for a walk together to see
the night-time animals."

Bunny couldn't wait to
go on his night-time adventure
and he bounced out of the burrow.
Outside, the sunset sky
was orange and pink.

"It's so beautiful," said Bunny.

"Keep close," Mummy said,
as she closed the front door.
"We need to stick together."

Bunny hopped close to Mummy for a while, but then,
he spotted something strange. With a hoppety-hop,
he went over to investigate.

There, lying among the flowers,
was a strange ball of prickles.
Bunny crouched down
and sniffed the prickly thing.

Suddenly, it uncurled.
A face and four paws popped out
and a little voice squeaked,
"Hello, I'm Hedgehog."

The hedgehog began
to roly-poly around on
the ground and Bunny
joined in. "This is fun!"
he giggled.

Then, Bunny rolled into Hedgehog and pricked his paw on the prickles. "Ouch, that hurt!" cried Bunny.

Mummy rubbed Bunny's paw.
"Never mind," she said, leading Bunny along the
woodland path. Soon, they came to a little
pond where a sleeping duck tucked
his beak under his wings.

The night was full of strange noises.
There were hoots and flutters and screeches and barks.
"What are those noises?" asked Bunny, nervously.
"They're night animals," replied Mummy.
"They're nothing to be afraid of."

Suddenly, a great, dark shape
swooped past Bunny. It was big
and feathery and made strange noises.
SWOOSH! TWIT-TWOO!

Little Bunny dived
into a patch of grass.
"Mummy, it's a monster!" he cried.

"Don't worry, Bunny,"
said Mummy.
"It's just the night owl.
He won't hurt you."

Bunny wasn't listening to Mummy.
He ran, hoppety-hoppety-hop
along the shadowy woodland path.
Suddenly, something black and white
and furry came out of a hole.

THUMP! Bunny bumped
straight into it.
"OUCH!" cried a very
grumpy badger.
"Watch where you're going!"

Bunny rubbed his sore nose.
His little ears drooped and
he felt sad. The night-time
animals didn't seem
friendly at all.

Just then, little fluttery bats flew past.
Bunny thought they looked very funny.
They whizzed between his ears
and round his fluffy, white tail.
Bunny giggled and chased
them round and round.

"Where are you,
Mummy?" called Bunny
from the wood.

Bunny felt so dizzy, he didn't
know which way was up.

He tried to hop, but he wibbled
and wobbled until he fell,
THUMP, right on his bottom.

Then, between the trees,
there was a flash of orange.
Something stepped out
into the moonlight.
It was a big, red,
bushy-tailed fox.

"Well, if it isn't a little bunny,"
said the sly fox, grinning.
"What are YOU doing out all
alone at this time of night?"

Suddenly, Mummy hopped
out from the trees. "He's being
a night-time bunny!" she cried.
The frightened fox leapt off into
the wood and Mummy
and Bunny were alone again.

"You mustn't run off
like that again, Bunny,"
said Mummy.

"Can we go home now?"
asked Bunny, sleepily.
"I'm tired and I want to go to bed."

"Okay," said Mummy,
giving him a cuddle.

"Let's go home then,"
she said. "I'll tuck you up so
you're snuggly and warm."

In his cosy, bunny bed,
inside the snuggly, bunny burrow,
Bunny thought about everything
he'd seen in the wood that night.

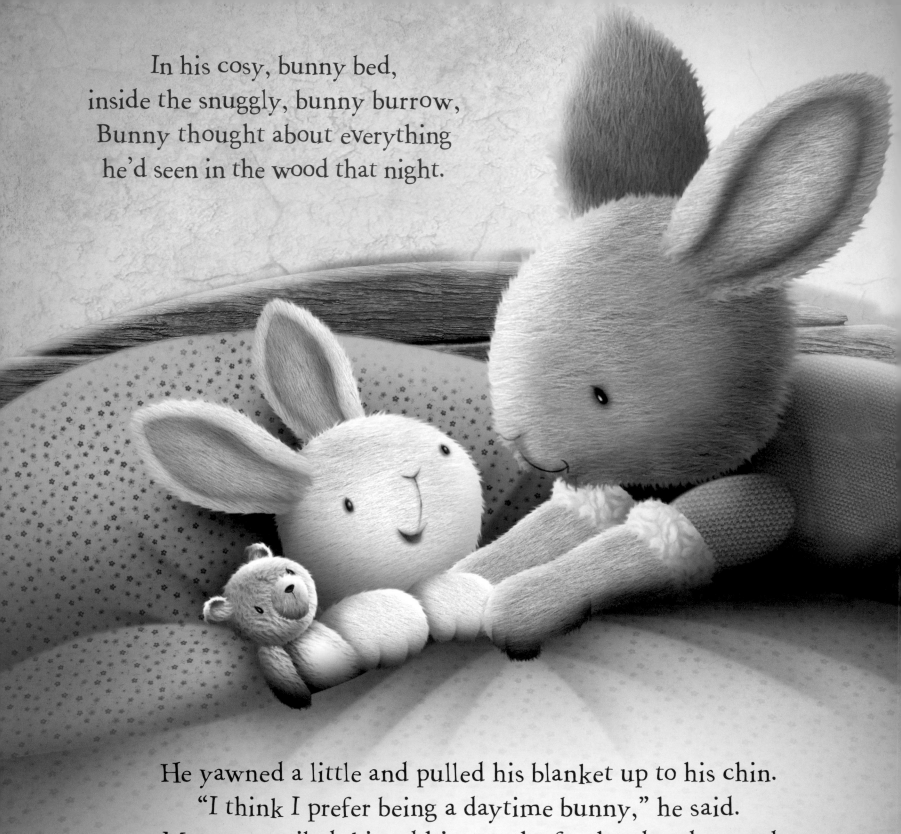

He yawned a little and pulled his blanket up to his chin.
"I think I prefer being a daytime bunny," he said.
Mummy smiled, kissed him on the forehead and turned
off his bedside light. "Sweet dreams, my little bunny."